Overcoming BULLYING

Learning to be NICE

Jasmine Brooke

FOX EYE
PUBLISHING

Zebra could be a little **MEAN** sometimes. She could be a little **CRUEL**.

Zebra often liked to **TEASE** her friends. She liked to **MAKE FUN** of them, too.

When Zebra was MEAN, she could be a BULLY. That was a problem at school.

One day, Peacock was painting a picture of himself and having a lot of fun. He thought his peacock tail looked especially beautiful, and being Peacock, he really felt rather proud.

Zebra had been watching Peacock, and she thought she'd have a little fun …

When Peacock said, "I've finished!" Zebra snorted, "Are you sure? It looks like you've only just begun!"

"That was **MEAN!**" cried Peacock. "I don't like you when you are **CRUEL!**" "Don't be silly," snorted Zebra. "I was just **MAKING FUN!**"

But what was fun for Zebra, wasn't fun for everyone.

In the afternoon, Mrs Tree asked Panther to read out loud. Panther tried very hard. He was doing so well, until he looked up and saw Zebra ... sticking out her tongue!

"Ooh, Zebra!" cried Wolf. "That was not a KIND thing to do." Then Bear growled, "I don't like it when you are CRUEL!"

The next day, Mrs Tree said that everyone could bake cakes.

Zebra watched as Peacock worked. She watched Panther trying hard. She saw Bear decorate her cake carefully, adding berries one by one.

Then Zebra did something only Zebra would find fun …

When Peacock wasn't looking, Zebra quickly ate a cake. When Panther was speaking to Mrs Tree, she quickly ate another. When Bear was washing her dishes, Zebra ate another two.

But Mrs Tree had been watching. "Zebra!" she cried. "That was not **KIND**."

Then Mrs Tree told Zebra, kindly, "**TEASING** can be **CRUEL**. Being **MEAN** is not kind. If **MAKING FUN** of others makes them sad, it's really not fun at all."

Zebra turned pink. She looked at the ground. Then she looked at Peacock, Panther and Bear.

"Now, Zebra," said Mrs Tree. "Let's try being **KIND**, and see how much fun that can be."

With Mrs Tree's help, Zebra baked and baked. Soon there were cakes for everyone, and Zebra was really having fun!

"I was **MEAN**," Zebra said to Peacock. "I was **CRUEL**," she told Panther. "I was a **BULLY**," Zebra said to Bear. "It's not a nice way to be."

Zebra had learnt not to be a **BULLY**. She had learnt to be **KIND**, and she had learnt it was a much nicer way to be.

Words and feelings

Zebra was a bully in this story and that made everyone around her feel upset.

TEASE

CRUEL

There are a lot of words to do with being mean in this book. Can you remember all of them?

MEAN

BULLY

MAKING FUN

Let's talk about behaviour

This series helps children to understand and manage difficult emotions and behaviours. The animal characters in the series have been created to show human behaviour that is often seen in young children, and which they may find difficult to manage.

Ocercoming Bullying

The story in this book examines issues around bullying. It looks at how being a bully upsets those around you and makes them dislike you, too.

The book is designed to show young children how they can manage their behaviour and learn to stop bullying.

How to use this book

You can read this book with one child or a group of children. The book can be used to begin a discussion around complex behaviour such as bullying.

The book is also a reading aid, with enlarged and repeated words to help children to develop their reading skills.

How to read the story

Before beginning the story, ensure that the children you are reading to are relaxed and focused.

Take time to look at the enlarged words and the illustrations, and discuss what this book might be about before reading the story.

New words can be tricky for young children to approach. Sounding them out first, slowly and repeatedly, can help children to learn the words and become familiar with them.

How to discuss the story

When you have finished reading the story, use these questions and discussion points to examine the theme of the story with children and explore the emotions and behaviours within it:

- What do you think the story was about? Have you been in a situation in which you were bullied or in which you bullied others? What was that situation? For example, did you make fun of a friend and upset them? Encourage the children to talk about their experiences.
- Talk about ways that people can learn to deal with bullying. For example, if you are tempted to be mean to someone and bully them, think about how you would feel if they did that to you. Talk to the children about what tools they think might work for them and why.
- Discuss what it is like when people bully. Explain that because Zebra was a bully, she upset her friends and that made them dislike her.
- Talk about why it is important to be kind to others and avoid bullying. Explain that bullies sometimes bully others because they feel unhappy. Explain that if everyone makes an effort not to bully, everyone, including the bullies, will feel happier.

Titles in the series

   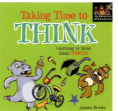 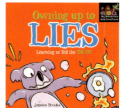
  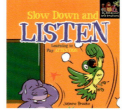 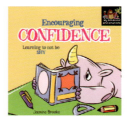 
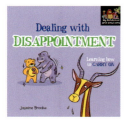   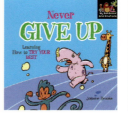 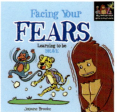
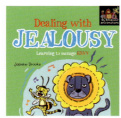  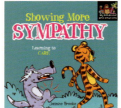  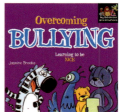

First published in 2023 by Fox Eye Publishing
Unit 31, Vulcan House Business Centre,
Vulcan Road, Leicester, LE5 3EF
www.foxeyepublishing.com

Copyright © 2023 Fox Eye Publishing
All rights reserved. No portion of this book may be reproduced in any form without permission from the publisher, except as permitted by U.K. copyright law.

Author: Jasmine Brooke
Art director: Paul Phillips
Cover designer: Emma Bailey & Salma Thadha
Editor: Jenny Rush

All illustrations by Novel

ISBN 978-1-80445-306-3

A catalogue record for this book is available from the British Library

Printed in China